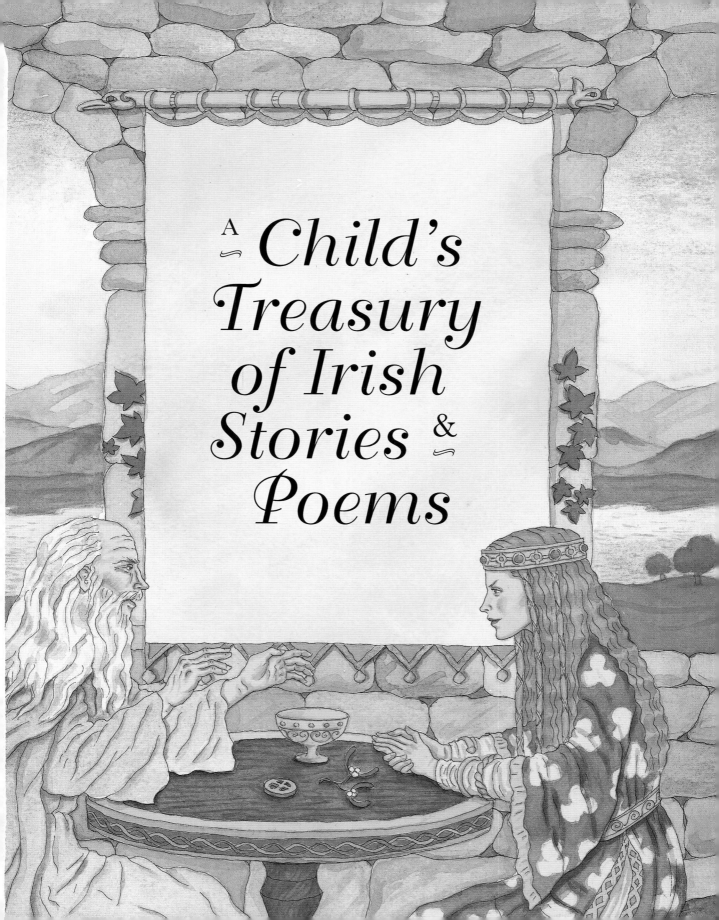

A Child's Treasury of Irish Stories & Poems

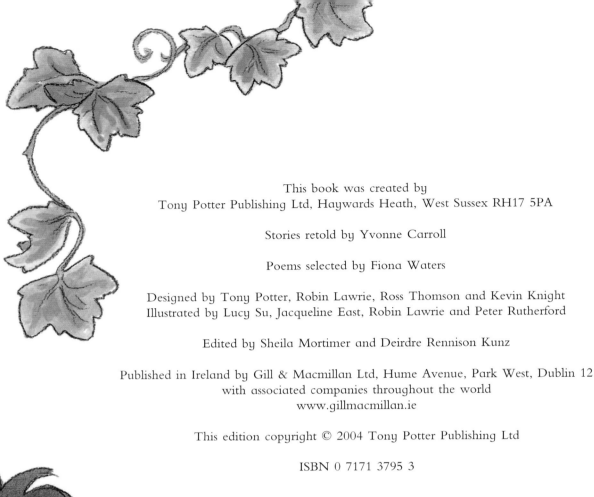

This book was created by
Tony Potter Publishing Ltd, Haywards Heath, West Sussex RH17 5PA

Stories retold by Yvonne Carroll

Poems selected by Fiona Waters

Designed by Tony Potter, Robin Lawrie, Ross Thomson and Kevin Knight
Illustrated by Lucy Su, Jacqueline East, Robin Lawrie and Peter Rutherford

Edited by Sheila Mortimer and Deirdre Rennison Kunz

Published in Ireland by Gill & Macmillan Ltd, Hume Avenue, Park West, Dublin 12
with associated companies throughout the world
www.gillmacmillan.ie

ISBN 0 7171 3795 3

Printed in Italy

13579108642

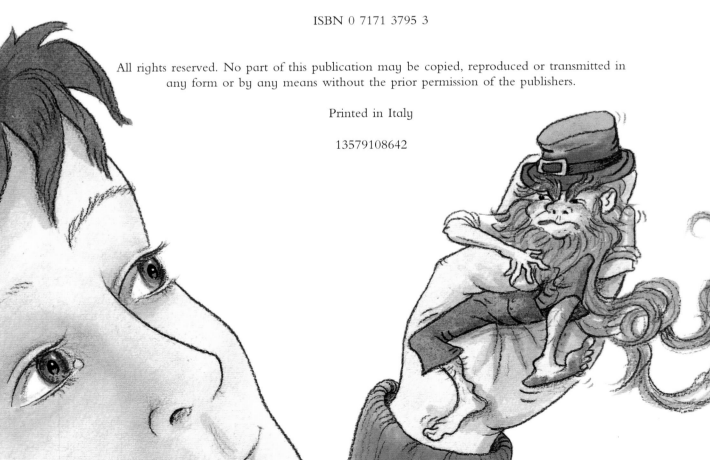

Contents

Introduction

Children of all ages will love this enchanting collection of tales, legends and poems. Drawing on hundreds of years of Irish folklore, there are tales of magic and mystery, of the mayhem caused by the "little people", together with stories of love and heroism, some familiar and some less so.

The mischievous exploits of wily leprechauns and their struggles to hang on to their pot of gold are recounted with humour and charm, while the extraordinary adventures of brave and courageous warriors vividly depict the perilous times in Irish history. There are mystical tales of children who dance with the fairies or become beautiful white swans, and cautionary stories telling what happens when humans ignore the "little people".

Interspersed throughout the anthology are poems ranging from the familiar and traditional Cockles and Mussels to the uproarious saga of Brian O'Linn – in fact, something for everyone to savour.

Beautifully illustrated throughout with lively and evocative images, this treasury of classic stories and poems is certain to become a favourite and cherished collection.

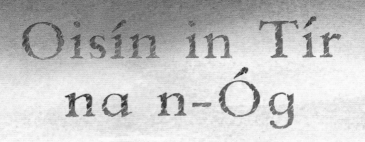

Oisín in Tír na n-Óg

One morning the Fianna were hunting deer on the shores of Loch Léin in Kerry. They saw a beautiful white horse coming towards them. Riding on the horse was the most beautiful woman they had ever seen. She wore a long dress as blue as the summer sky, studded with silver stars, and her long golden hair hung to her waist.

"What is your name and what land have you come from?" asked Fionn, leader of the Fianna.
"I am Niamh of the golden hair. My father is king of Tír na n-Óg," she replied. "I have heard of a warrior called Oisín. I have heard of his courage and of his poetry. I have come to find him and take him back with me to Tír na n-Óg."

Oisín was the son of Fionn. He
was a great hero and a poet.
"Tell me," Oisín said, "what sort
of a land is Tír na n-Óg?"

"Tír na n-Óg is the land of youth," replied Niamh. "It is a happy place, with no pain or sorrow. Any wish you make comes true and no one grows old there. If you come with me, you will find out all this is true."

Oisín mounted the white horse and said goodbye to his father and friends. He promised he would return soon. The horse galloped off over the water, moving as swiftly as a shadow. The Fianna were sad to see their hero go, but Fionn reminded them of Oisín's promise to return soon.

The king and queen of Tír na
n-Óg welcomed Oisín and held
a great feast in his honour. It was
indeed a wonderful land, just as
Niamh had said. He hunted and
feasted and at night he told
stories of Fionn and the Fianna
and of their lives in Ireland.
Oisín had never felt as happy as
he did with Niamh and before
long they were married.

Time passed quickly and although
he was very happy, Oisín began
to think of returning home for a
visit. Niamh didn't want him to
go, but at last she said:
"Take my white horse. It will
carry you safely to Ireland and
back. Whatever happens, you
must not get off the horse and
touch the soil of Ireland. If you do,
you will never return to me or to
Tír na n-Óg."

She did not tell him that although
he thought he'd only been away
a few years, he had really been
there three hundred years.

Ireland seemed a strange place to
Oisín when he arrived back.
There seemed to be no trace of
his father or the rest of the
Fianna. The people he saw
seemed small and weak to him.

As he passed through Gleann na
Smól, he saw some men trying
to move a large stone.
"I will help you," said Oisín. The
men were terrified of this giant on
a white horse. Stooping from his
saddle, Oisín lifted the stone with
one hand and hurled it. With that,
the saddle girth broke and Oisín
was flung to the ground.

Immediately the white horse
disappeared and the men saw
before them an old, old man.
They took him to a holy man
who lived nearby.

"Where are my father and the Fianna?" Oisín asked. When he was told that they were long dead, he was heartbroken. He spoke of the many deeds of Fionn and the Fianna and their adventures together. He spoke of his time in Tír na n-Óg and his beautiful wife that he would not see again. Although he died soon after, the wonderful stories of Oisín have lived on.

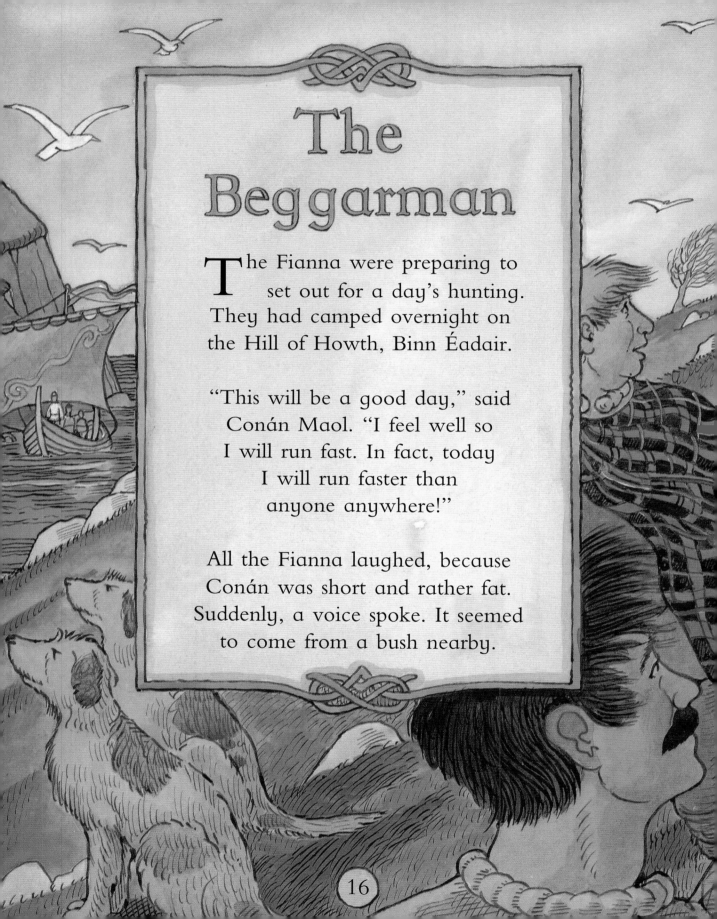

The Beggarman

The Fianna were preparing to set out for a day's hunting. They had camped overnight on the Hill of Howth, Binn Éadair.

"This will be a good day," said Conán Maol. "I feel well so I will run fast. In fact, today I will run faster than anyone anywhere!"

All the Fianna laughed, because Conán was short and rather fat. Suddenly, a voice spoke. It seemed to come from a bush nearby.

"Fast! You, run fast! Rubbish!
No one could outrun me."
With that, a strange-looking sight
appeared from the bushes and
stood before the Fianna. It was an
old beggarman dressed in a long,
tattered coat that reached the
ground. On his feet he wore
enormous boots that were so
caked with mud that he could
barely lift his feet to walk.

17

While this was happening, no one noticed a ship sailing into the bay, nor had they noticed the warrior who had jumped ashore and was striding across the beach towards them. As he walked, his golden helmet glistened in the sunlight and his purple cloak blew out behind him.

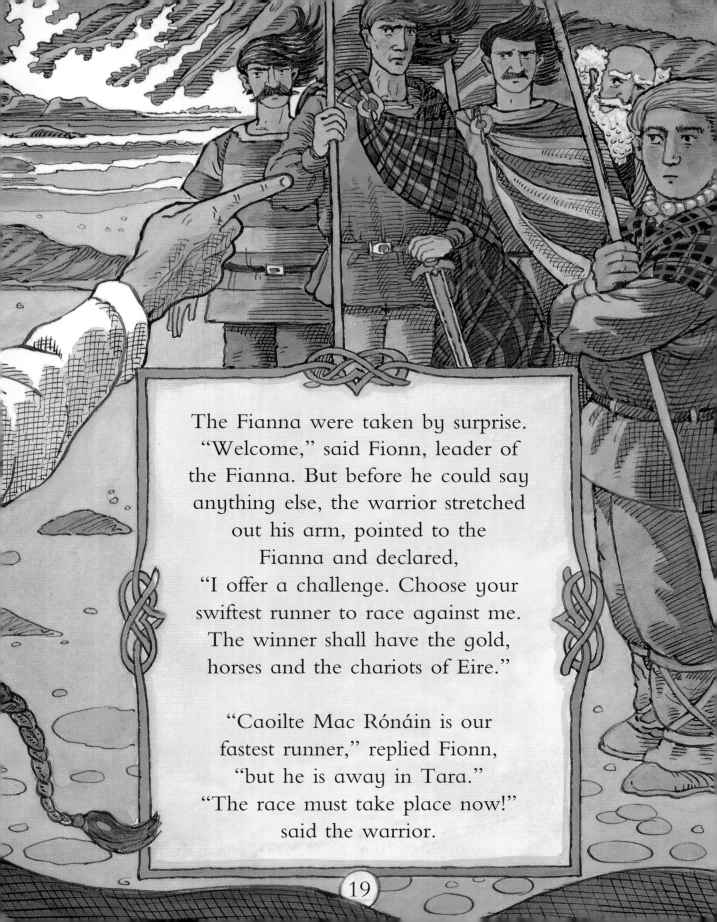

The Fianna were taken by surprise.
"Welcome," said Fionn, leader of
the Fianna. But before he could say
anything else, the warrior stretched
out his arm, pointed to the
Fianna and declared,
"I offer a challenge. Choose your
swiftest runner to race against me.
The winner shall have the gold,
horses and the chariots of Eire."

"Caoilte Mac Rónáin is our
fastest runner," replied Fionn,
"but he is away in Tara."
"The race must take place now!"
said the warrior.

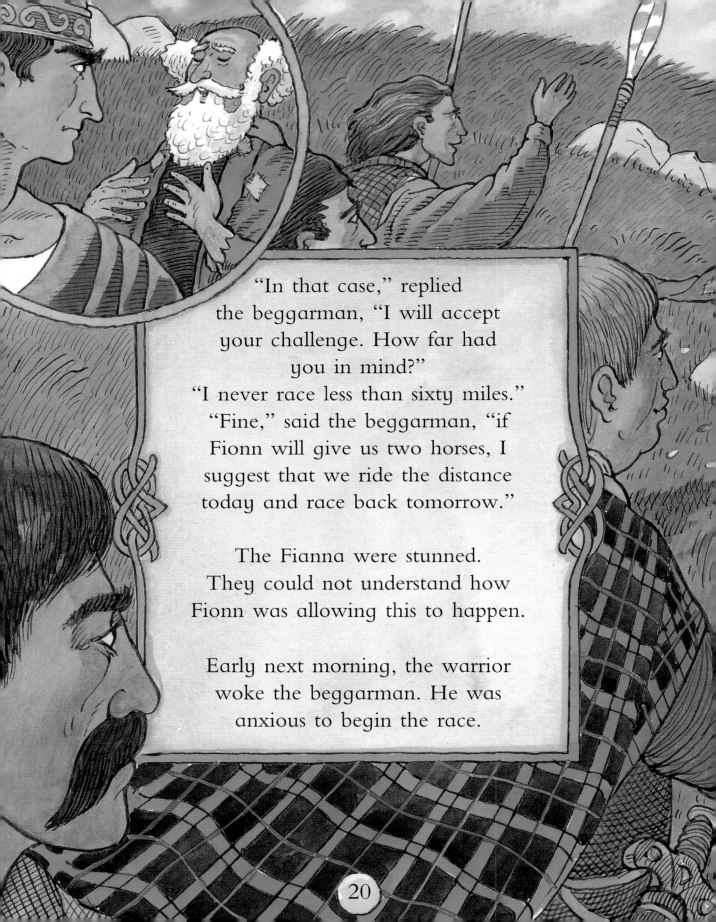

"In that case," replied the beggarman, "I will accept your challenge. How far had you in mind?"
"I never race less than sixty miles."
"Fine," said the beggarman, "if Fionn will give us two horses, I suggest that we ride the distance today and race back tomorrow."

The Fianna were stunned. They could not understand how Fionn was allowing this to happen.

Early next morning, the warrior woke the beggarman. He was anxious to begin the race.

"I would never dream of running
this early. If you are in such a
rush, you set off and I will follow
you later," said the beggarman
and, curling up, he fell asleep.
When he finally woke it was
mid-morning. He set off to catch
up with the warrior.

21

What a sight he was, the tails of
his long coat flapping in the wind
behind him as he jumped and
hopped but never ran. But it
wasn't long before he had caught
up with the warrior.

"We are halfway there now,"
said the beggarman.
"Have you stopped to eat yet?"
There was no answer so he
raced on ahead.
"Well, I am hungry and
I must eat," he muttered
to himself.

The bushes around were thick
with ripe, juicy blackberries. The
beggarman began to gobble
them in fistfuls. By the time the
warrior caught up with him, his
coat and face were purple with
blackberry juice.

"The tails of your coat are caught
up in the bush ten miles back,"
snarled the warrior.
"Oh dear," said the beggarman,
"it would never do for me to lose
them!" Running backwards
he found them, and with three
long hops and a jump caught
up with the warrior again.

Meanwhile, Fionn and the Fianna were waiting on the top of Binn Éadair.
"Do you see anyone coming?" they asked each other.
"I can see something in the distance," whispered Conán Maol.

At the sight of the beggarman the Fianna gave a great cheer of joy and relief. But as they gathered round him, they heard the fearsome roar of the warrior as he approached with his sword drawn. He swung the blade of the sword at the beggarman; but when the Fianna looked, the warrior's head was rolling by the beggarman's side.

"Let that be a lesson to you," said the beggarman. "It's a lucky day for you that I'm feeling generous!"
With that he reached down, picked up the head and threw it back on the warrior's shoulders where it landed back to front!

"Our thanks to you, my friend," said Fionn. "You have saved the honour of the Fianna and I now know who you really are."

Turning to his men Fionn said, "This is the prince from Tír na n-Óg. Once a year he becomes human." "I have enjoyed my time with you but now I must return to my own people," said the beggarman.

He raised his arms to wave and, as he did, his appearance changed and there before them stood a tall, fair-haired prince.

As they watched, a white mist surrounded him and when it cleared he had disappeared, leaving them alone on the Hill of Howth.

The Crock of Gold

It was a clear moonlit night as Tom walked home from the village. Suddenly he heard a most peculiar sound coming from the bushes ahead. His mother had warned him to ignore strange sounds at night, as this was when the fairy people appeared. Even so, Tom paused for a moment before moving closer to the bushes to see what could possibly be making the noise.

He couldn't believe his eyes! There
in front of him was a little man
no bigger than Tom's hand,
with his beard tangled in the bush.
He wore brown trousers, a green
waistcoat and a bright red cap on
his head and his tiny shoes were on
the ground beside him. He had
something in his hand and when
Tom looked at it closely he saw
that it was an awl the size
of a thimble.

"This is my lucky day!" Tom thought to himself. "I have found a leprechaun and every leprechaun has a pot of gold. I just have to keep him in sight and the gold will be mine."

Tom grabbed the leprechaun. He struggled, but Tom held him tightly and untangled his beard. This made the little man angry, but Tom ignored his bad temper and whistled a merry tune. All the while he made sure that he kept a firm hold on the leprechaun.

"Put me down," he shouted. "Not until you tell me where you have hidden your crock of gold," replied Tom. At last, when the leprechaun realised that Tom was determined not to let him go, he said, "Right, I give up. The gold is buried under this bush. Now let me go."

"Oh no!" said Tom. "I have no spade and if I go home now, how will I remember which bush is the one with the gold?"

"Why not mark the bush with your handkerchief?" suggested the leprechaun. "Of course!" agreed Tom, "but you must promise me that you won't take the gold when I'm gone."

The leprechaun promised, so Tom put him down and set off home.

The dawn was breaking by the time Tom returned. As he approached the bushes, what a sight met his eyes! Every bush had a bright red handkerchief tied to its lowest branch. "What a fool I was to let the leprechaun out of my sight," he whispered sadly to himself. "The gold will never be mine now."

Perhaps he imagined it, but as he slowly made his way home, Tom thought he could hear the sound of laughter blowing on the wind.

A Ballad of Master McGrath

Eighteen sixty nine being the date of the year,
Those Waterloo sportsmen and more did appear
For to gain the great prizes and bear them awa',
Never counting on Ireland and Master McGrath.

On the 12th of December, that day of renown,
McGrath and his keeper they left Lurgan town;
A gale in the Channel, it soon drove them o'er,
On the thirteenth they landed on fair England's shore.

And when they arrived there in big London town,
Those great English sportsmen they all gathered
    round –
And some of the gentlemen gave a "Ha! Ha!"
Saying: "Is that the great dog you call
    Master McGrath?"

And one of those gentlemen standing around
Says: "I don't care a damn for your Irish
    greyhound";
And another he laughs with a scornful "Ha! Ha!
We'll soon humble the pride of your Master
    McGrath."

Then Lord Lurgan came forward and said: "Gentlemen,
If there's any amongst you has money to spend –
For you nobles of England I don't care a straw –
Here's five thousand to one upon Master
        McGrath."

Then McGrath he looked up and he wagged his
        old tail,
Informing his lordship, "I know what you mane,
Don't fear, noble Brownlow, don't fear them, agra,
For I'll tarnish their laurels," says Master McGrath.

And Rose stood uncovered, the great English
        pride,
Her master and keeper were close by her side;
They have let her away and the crowd cried,
        "Hurrah!"
For the pride of all England – and Master
        McGrath.

As Rose and the Master they both ran along,
"Now I wonder," says Rose, "what took you from
    your home;
You should have stopped there in your Irish
    demesne,
And not come to gain laurels on Albion's plain."

"Well, I know," says McGrath, "we have wild
    heather bogs,
But you'll find in old Ireland there's good men
    and dogs.
Lead on, bold Britannia, give none of your jaw,
Snuff that up your nostrils," says Master McGrath.

Then the hare she went on just as swift as
    the wind,
He was sometime before her and sometime
    behind.
Rose gave the first turn according to law;
But the second was given by Master McGrath.

The hare she led on with a wonderful view,
And swift as the wind o'er the green field
    she flew.
But he jumped on her back and he held up
    his paw
"Three cheers for old Ireland," says Master McGrath.

Anonymous

Deirdre of the Sorrows

When the baby Deirdre was born, her father, Feidhlim, asked the wise druids to look at the stars and tell him what the future held for her.

The wise druids answered: "This baby will cause great trouble. She will grow up to be the most beautiful woman in Ulster, but she will cause the death of many of our men."

When the Red Branch Knights of
Ulster heard this, they were very
worried for their lives. They went
to King Connor demanding that
baby Deirdre be killed.

The king thought for a while.
"I have the answer," he said.
"Deirdre will be brought up far
away from here and when she is
old enough I will marry her."

43

Deirdre was taken away at once to a deep wood. The king chose a wise old woman, called Leabharcham, to care for her and teach her. As Deirdre grew older she became as beautiful as the druids had foretold. She had long golden hair and deep blue eyes. However, she was a very lonely girl.

One day, Deirdre told
Leabharcham about a dream she
had every night.
"I dream of a tall dark warrior.
His hair is as black as the
raven. His skin is as white
as snow. He is
fearless in battle."
Leabharcham was
worried as she knew
the man Deirdre
dreamt about.
"He is Naoise, one
of the Sons of
Uisneach.
You must never
mention your dream
again. You will be
married to King
Connor very soon,"
she said.

45

Deirdre begged Leabharcham to
send for Naoise so she might meet
the man of her dreams.

At first Leabharcham refused but
she hated to see Deirdre unhappy
and she gave in. Deirdre and
Naoise met and they fell in love
at once.

"We must go far away from Ulster now," said Deirdre. "I cannot marry Connor."

Deirdre, Naoise and his brothers Áinle and Ardan set off. They travelled all around Ireland but no one would help them because they all feared the anger of King Connor. Finally they sailed to a small island off the coast of Scotland.

There they lived for some time
until one day a messenger
arrived from the king. He
reported that King Connor had
forgiven them.

Deirdre did not trust the message
but the Sons of Uisneach
believed it. Reluctantly, Deirdre
set off with them to Ireland.

On the way she pleaded with
them to turn back but they
would not listen.

When they arrived they were sent to the house of the Red Branch Knights, not the king's castle. Now Deirdre was sure that a trap had been set for them.

Deirdre was right. Soon the house was surrounded. The Sons of Uisneach fought bravely but they were outnumbered. They were seized and brought before Connor. "Who will kill these traitors for me?" asked the king.
None of the Red Branch Knights would kill a fellow knight. Suddenly an unknown warrior from another kingdom stepped forward.
"I will kill them," he shouted. With one blow he cut off the heads of the Sons of Uisneach.

Deirdre screamed and fell dying
to the ground beside the body of
Naoise. So great was her sorrow
that her heart had broken.

Deirdre's father was so angry with
Connor that he left Ulster and
went to live in Connacht. Many
other warriors went with him and
joined the army of Queen Maeve.
This army was later to fight
bloody battles against the Red
Branch Knights.

So Deirdre did bring sorrow and
trouble to Ulster just as the druids
had foretold.

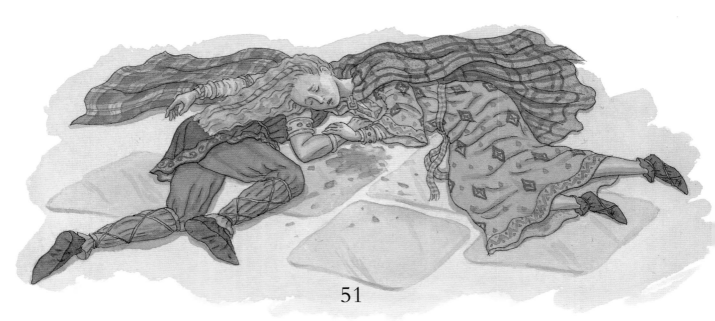

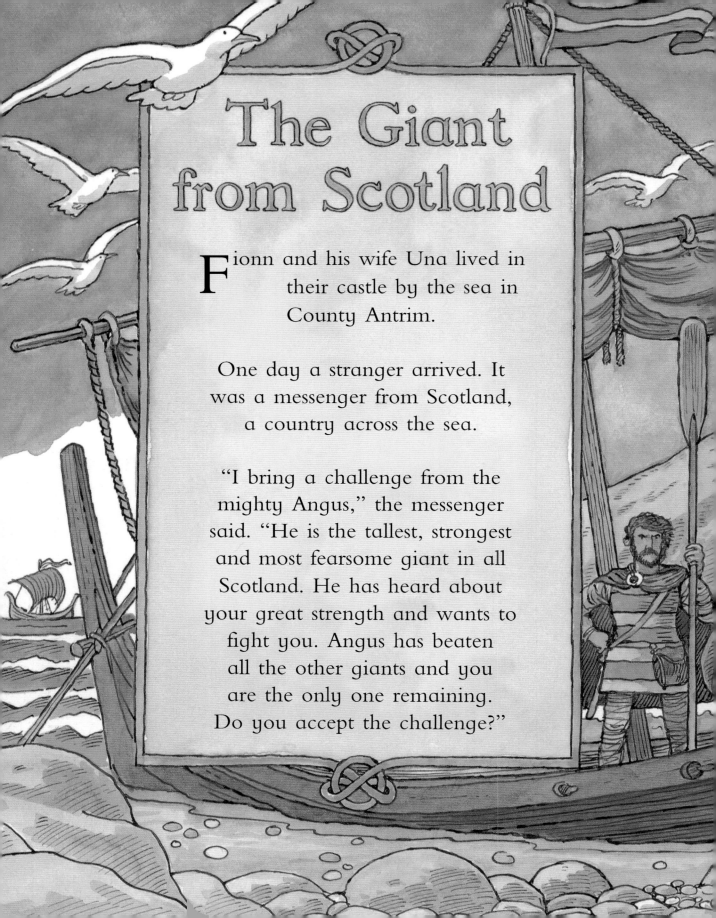

The Giant from Scotland

Fionn and his wife Una lived in their castle by the sea in County Antrim.

One day a stranger arrived. It was a messenger from Scotland, a country across the sea.

"I bring a challenge from the mighty Angus," the messenger said. "He is the tallest, strongest and most fearsome giant in all Scotland. He has heard about your great strength and wants to fight you. Angus has beaten all the other giants and you are the only one remaining. Do you accept the challenge?"

"Of course I accept," said Fionn.
"I will begin to prepare
immediately." And so he did!

From that day on, Fionn worked hard. He had decided to build a path across the sea to Scotland. It was a rather unusual causeway made up of hundreds of thousands of black rocks, all of different sizes and different heights. Some rocks had six sides, some eight and others more than ten sides.

The warriors of the Fianna looked on in amazement as Fionn worked each day. Before long the causeway stretched miles into the sea.

One evening when Fionn
returned home he noticed
that Una was worried.
"What is the matter?" he asked.
"Oh Fionn," she replied, "I heard
some very disturbing news today.
I heard that Angus is indeed
much bigger than you and that
he is definitely stronger."

"If I cannot beat him with my
strength, then we must think
of a plan," Fionn said, "I may not
be as big or as strong as he is,
but I am much cleverer."

Fionn and Una talked for many
hours. They thought of many
plans, but could not find one that
they were sure would work.
Time was running out.
Later that week the messenger
from Angus returned and told
Fionn that Angus would arrive
in two days' time.

"Tell him that Fionn is ready
and waiting," said Una.
"Do not worry, Fionn,
I have a plan in mind."

Una worked hard for the next
two days. She spent the time
cutting and sewing and knitting.
"Imagine sewing and knitting at
a time like this!" he exclaimed.
"I thought you had a plan."

"Look carefully," said Una.
"What do you see?"
Fionn was amazed.
"Clothes," he said. "I see clothes,
but they are most peculiar!"

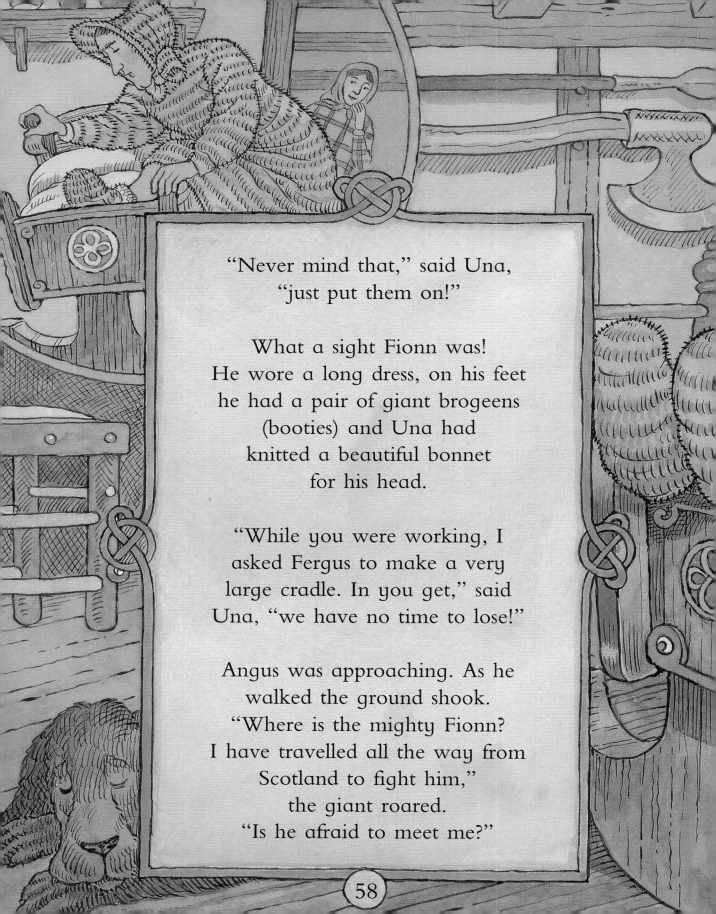

"Never mind that," said Una,
"just put them on!"

What a sight Fionn was!
He wore a long dress, on his feet
he had a pair of giant brogeens
(booties) and Una had
knitted a beautiful bonnet
for his head.

"While you were working, I
asked Fergus to make a very
large cradle. In you get," said
Una, "we have no time to lose!"

Angus was approaching. As he
walked the ground shook.
"Where is the mighty Fionn?
I have travelled all the way from
Scotland to fight him,"
the giant roared.
"Is he afraid to meet me?"

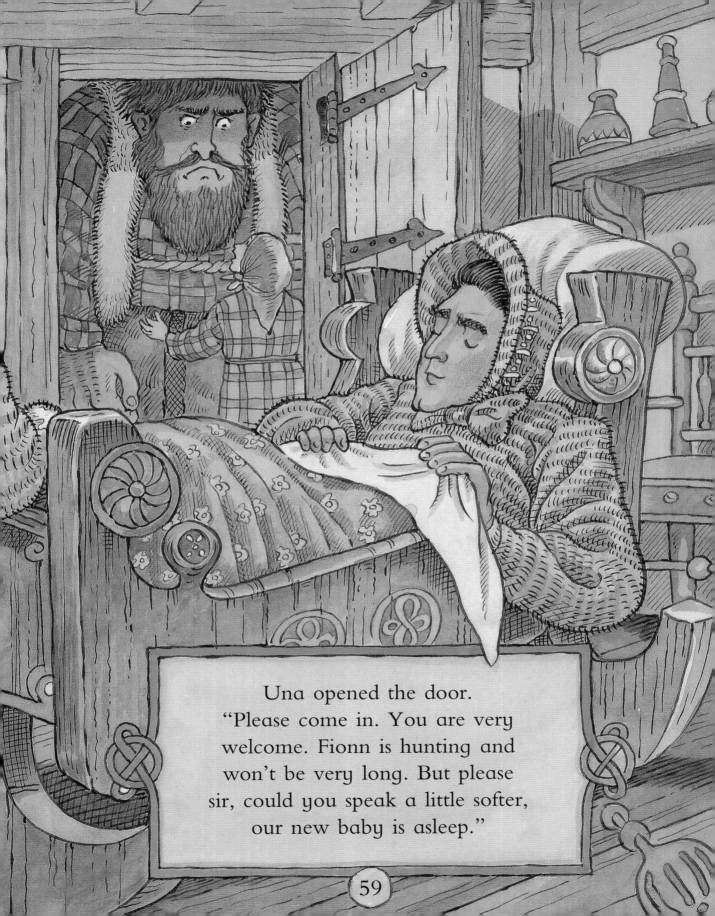

Una opened the door.
"Please come in. You are very
welcome. Fionn is hunting and
won't be very long. But please
sir, could you speak a little softer,
our new baby is asleep."

"That is your baby?"
Angus gasped in shock.
"Yes, he is rather small now,
but he will grow," replied Una.
Angus was frightened. He had
never seen a baby this big.
"If this is Fionn's small baby,
what size is Fionn?" he wondered.
"Fionn himself must be enormous!"

Angus hurried out and,
without turning, he ran
across the causeway.

As he was running, a thought
struck him. "What if Fionn is
following me?" To prevent this
happening, he began to remove
stones from the path and, by
the time he arrived home to
Scotland, all that was left
was a few yards of the path jutting
out from the coast of Antrim
into the sea. To this day, only that
part of the causeway remains.

All Things Bright and Beautiful

All things bright and beautiful,
All creatures great and small,
All things wise and wonderful,
The Lord God made them all.

Each little flower that opens,
Each little bird that sings,
He made their glowing colours,
He made their tiny wings.

The purple-headed mountain,
The river running by,
The sunset, and the morning,
That brightens up the sky;

The cold wind in the winter,
The pleasant summer sun,
The ripe fruits in the garden
He made them every one.

The tall trees in the greenwood,
The meadows where we play,
The rushes by the water
We gather every day.

He gave us eyes to see them,
And lips that we might tell,
How great is God Almighty,
Who has made all things well.

Cecil Frances Alexander

The Sidhe

Once upon a time, a man called Sean lived in a small cottage near a small village. During the long winter nights the people of the village used to meet and tell stories or sing to pass the time. Sean loved the music and the stories, but unlike his family and neighbours he didn't believe in fairies or leprechauns or any of the little people. In fact, whenever he heard anyone talk about the Sidhe he would laugh and say that he couldn't understand how anyone could be so foolish as to believe that such stories could possibly be true.

One warm summer day, Sean was
resting by the edge of his field.
The air was filled with various
sounds. He heard birds chirping
and busy bees humming as they
collected pollen. Suddenly, he
became aware of another sound. It
was a gentle tap-tapping which
seemed to come from a nearby
hedge. Sean moved forward
slowly to investigate.

He couldn't believe what he saw before him! It was a real live leprechaun, exactly like those that Sean said didn't exist. The little man was there in front of him, sitting on a mushroom working hard. At his feet lay many different shoes, some with buckles, some dainty fairy slippers and some boots.

In a flash, Sean reached out and grabbed the little man. "Where is your pot of gold?" he demanded. "Gold!" said the little man crossly. "Gold! Where would I get a pot of gold? I'm only a poor shoemaker. All I have are my tools and this piece of leather."

"You can't fool me," said Sean.
"Give me your gold and I'll set you
free." "All right!" the little man
cried. "My gold is buried safely in
the field by the river. Take me
there and I'll show you."

From the stories he had heard, Sean knew exactly what he had to do to get the leprechaun to part with his gold. He must not take his eyes off the man for an instant.

The leprechaun led him to a bush near the water's edge, in the next field. "There you are," he cried. "Take my gold." Keeping his eyes on the leprechaun, Sean reached into the bush. Suddenly he gave a scream of pain, for instead of a pot of gold he had put his hand into a bee hive!

Of course he looked to see where the bees were. As soon as Sean had taken his eyes off him, the little man vanished, just as the stories said he would.

Sean never told anyone how the leprechaun had fooled him when it was his turn to tell a story during the long winter nights. But no-one ever again heard him say that he didn't believe in fairies or leprechauns.

Cockles and Mussels

In Dublin's fair city,
Where the girls are so pretty,
    I first set my eyes on sweet Mollie Malone,
She wheeled her wheel-barrow
Through streets broad and narrow,
    Crying, "Cockles and mussels, alive, alive, oh!
        Alive, alive, oh! Alive, alive, oh!"
        Crying, "Cockles and mussels, alive, alive, oh!"

She was a fishmonger.
But sure 'twas no wonder,
    For so were her father and mother before.
And they both wheeled their barrow
Through streets broad and narrow,
    Crying, "Cockles and mussels, alive, alive, oh!
        Alive, alive, oh! Alive, alive, oh!"
        Crying, "Cockles and mussels, alive, alive, oh!"

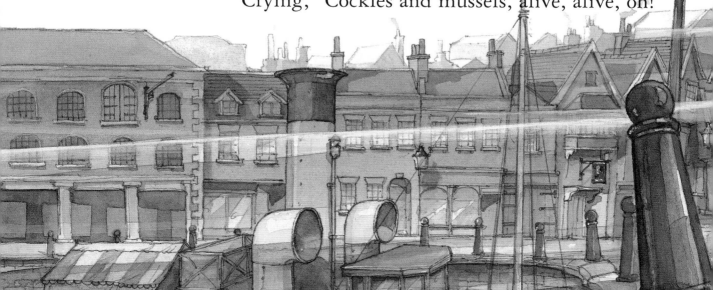

She died of a fever,
And none could relieve her,
    And that was the end of sweet Mollie Malone.
But her ghost wheels her barrow
Through streets broad and narrow,
    Crying, "Cockles and mussels, alive, alive, oh!
      Alive, alive, oh! Alive, alive, oh!"
              Crying, "Cockles and mussels,
                    alive, alive, oh!"

Anonymous

The Salmon
of Knowledge

Long ago in Ireland the king had a special army of soldiers called the Fianna to guard him. Cumhall was their most famous leader. His enemies were jealous of him, so they killed him. Cumhall's wife was afraid that her young son Fionn might also be killed.

So she took him to two women
warriors who lived on the slopes
of the Sliabh Bloom Mountains.
She asked the women to teach the
young boy all that a son of
Cumhall should know, for she
knew that some day her son
would become one of the Fianna.

At that time, any youth wishing
to join the Fianna had to pass
very difficult tests. He had to
defend himself against the spears
of nine men using only a shield;
he had to jump over a pole as
high as his head; and he had to
recite twelve books of poetry.

When the women had taught
Fionn all the fighting skills he
would need, they sent him to
Finnéigeas the poet, to learn the
twelve books of poetry.

Finnéigeas lived on the banks of the river Boyne. He had spent many years living beside this river and fishing in it. There was a fish in the Boyne known as the Salmon of Knowledge. The person who caught and ate it would know everything there was to know in the world. Finnéigeas liked the young fair-haired Fionn and agreed to become his teacher.

One day as Fionn was learning
poetry he heard a shout.
He rushed to the river and
there stood Finnéigeas holding
a large salmon.
"Take the fish and cook it for
me, please, Fionn," he said.
"Remember you must not eat
any of it."

Fionn did as he was told. He cleaned the salmon, lit the fire and put the salmon over the fire to cook. All was well until a blister rose on the side of the salmon. Without thinking, Fionn reached out and broke the skin of the blister. In doing so he burnt his thumb and sucked it to stop the pain. He finished cooking the fish as Finnéigeas returned.

The old man looked at Fionn
and saw in his eyes the
knowledge he had spent so many
years searching for.
"There is nothing for me to teach
you now," he said sadly. "You
must go to Tara and take your
father's place at the head of the
Fianna. Always use your
knowledge wisely."

Fionn set off at once to join the
Fianna. From then on, whenever
he had a problem, all he had to
do was to put his thumb in his
mouth and he had the answer
at once.

The Magic Cloak

It was almost dawn. Both sea and land were covered in mist. Eoin hid behind the rock as the tide ebbed far out into the bay. He had been waiting a long time for this special day. Every seven years a very strange magical event happened.

The old people in the village said that the sea went out as far as the horizon and the fairy people appeared. They spread a magic cloak in the centre of the sands and this held back the tide. Whoever owned the cloak could order the sea to stay back and would have good fertile land to make a farm.

Eoin always listened carefully to the stories the old people told, especially this one. Seven years earlier, he had crept out and watched in amazement as the waves rolled back and the fairy people appeared! This time he waited with his horse tethered nearby. At dawn they came. Eoin could hear the music of the fiddles and harps. Through the mist he could barely make out the shadows.

Slowly he got on his horse, making sure not to startle the animal. The mist lifted and once again Eoin saw the strangest sight before his eyes. The sea and sand had disappeared and in its place was a green plain as far as he could see.

Eoin knew what to do. He had to get the magic cloak — and the land would be his! But the cloak was guarded by leprechauns. He soon spotted them sitting in a circle, a pile of tiny shoes at their feet, tapping in time to the music. They were sitting on the cloak and the edges were flapping in the breeze.

Eoin pulled gently on the reins of
his horse as they moved forwards.
It took him longer than he
expected to reach the cloak. When
he looked back, it seemed that the
shoreline was very far away
in the distance.

As he came near to the leprechauns he slowed his horse and then dismounted a short distance away. He crept forward. He thought that they must hear his heart thumping or the sound of his breathing but no, they continued to work.

He reached out and, taking hold of a corner of the cloak, he pulled it from under them. Without delay he threw the cloak on his back, mounted his horse and galloped towards the shore. He could hear the chaos and confusion behind him but he dared not look back.

93

Suddenly all was quiet. It was an eerie quiet. The breeze dropped. "I've made it!" Eoin thought. Then he heard a rumbling noise. He looked over his shoulder and moving towards him with terrific speed was a gigantic wave. It was the Fairy Wave! Eoin urged his horse on but he was swept from the saddle. He felt as if he was being pulled in many directions and beaten by many pairs of hands.

As quickly as it had come the wave disappeared. When Eoin woke and tried to move, every bone and muscle in his body ached. "I've survived the Fairy Wave," he thought. "I have the magic cloak. I can control the sea. I'll be rich. I have beaten the fairies. I don't mind the pain." He put his hand on his back to feel the cloak but instead all he felt was a cloak of seaweed.

The Leprahaun

In a shady nook one moonlit night,
　　A leprahaun I spied
In scarlet coat and cap of green,
　　A cruiskeen by his side.
'Twas tick, tack, tick, his hammer went,
　　Upon a weeny shoe,
And I laughed to think of a purse of gold,
　　But the fairy was laughing too.

With tip-toe step and beating heart,
　　Quite softly I drew nigh.
There was mischief in his merry face,
　　A twinkle in his eye;
He hammered and sang with tiny voice,
　　And sipped the mountain dew;
Oh! I laughed to think he was caught at last,
　　But the fairy was laughing, too.

As quick as thought I grasped the elf,
  "Your fairy purse," I cried,
"My purse?" said he, " 'tis in her hand,
  That lady by your side."
I turned to look, the elf was off,
  And what was I to do?
Oh! I laughed to think what a fool I'd been,
  And the fairy was laughing too.

Robert Dwyer Joyce

Oisín

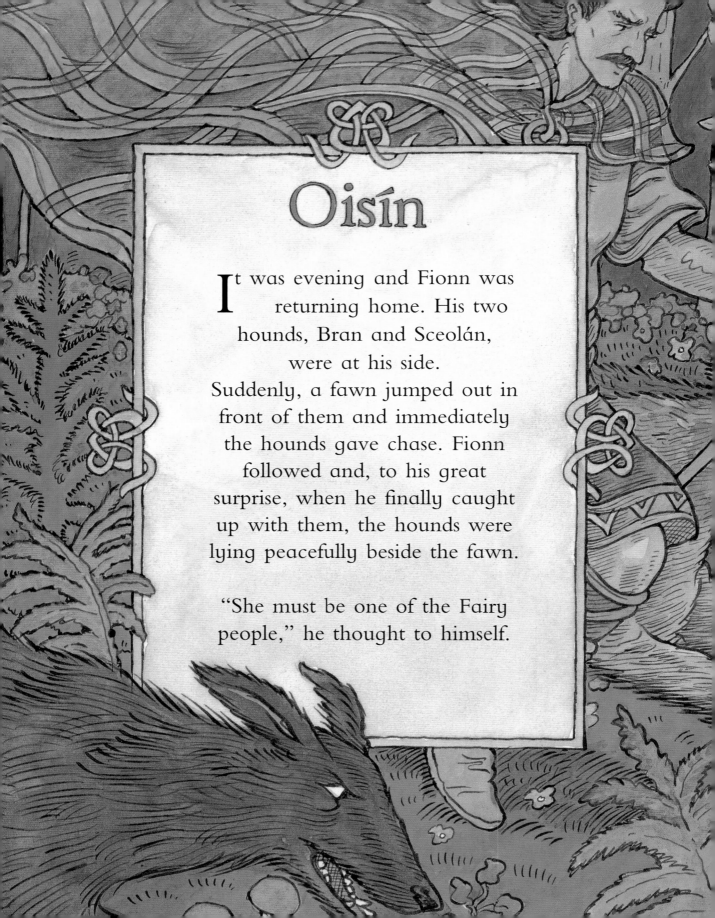

It was evening and Fionn was returning home. His two hounds, Bran and Sceolán, were at his side. Suddenly, a fawn jumped out in front of them and immediately the hounds gave chase. Fionn followed and, to his great surprise, when he finally caught up with them, the hounds were lying peacefully beside the fawn.

"She must be one of the Fairy people," he thought to himself.

During the night Fionn woke to find a beautiful young girl standing at his bedside. He knew that she must be the fawn he had hunted that day.

"I need your help, Fionn," she whispered softly. "My name is Sadhb, and you are the only one who can help me. Two years ago, one of the druids of my people, the Fear Dorcha, wanted me to be his wife. When I refused, he cast a spell on me and turned me into a fawn. Only the man I love can protect me."

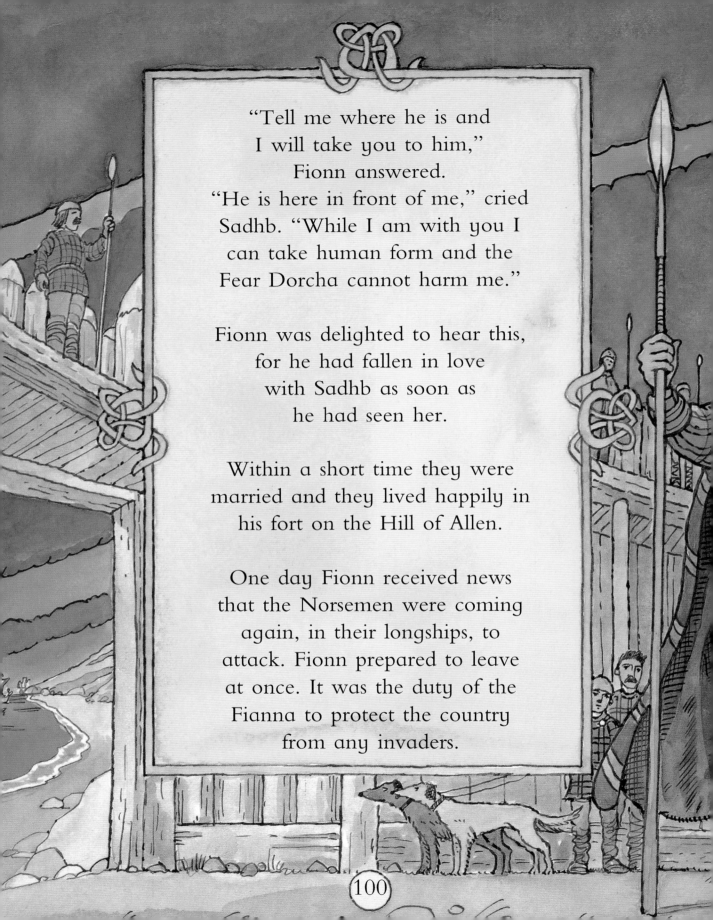

"Tell me where he is and
I will take you to him,"
Fionn answered.
"He is here in front of me," cried
Sadhb. "While I am with you I
can take human form and the
Fear Dorcha cannot harm me."

Fionn was delighted to hear this,
for he had fallen in love
with Sadhb as soon as
he had seen her.

Within a short time they were
married and they lived happily in
his fort on the Hill of Allen.

One day Fionn received news
that the Norsemen were coming
again, in their longships, to
attack. Fionn prepared to leave
at once. It was the duty of the
Fianna to protect the country
from any invaders.

Before leaving he warned Sadhb not to venture outside the fort until he returned. The fight was long and difficult, but eventually the invaders were driven back to their ships. Immediately, Fionn set off for home.

As Fionn approached the fort he was troubled. He could see no sign of Sadhb coming to greet him. Then he grew fearful and rushed into the fort.

His chief steward came to him and told him terrible news. "One morning as Sadhb looked over the plain, she gave a great shout of joy. She cried out that you were returning. We looked out and we saw you with Bran and Sceolán, but were surprised that none of your warriors was with you. Before anyone could say a word, Sadhb ran out to welcome you home."

"As she drew near you, she realised that it wasn't you, but the Fear Dorcha. We were powerless, and could only watch helplessly as he touched her with a hazel rod and she became a fawn. She tried to escape but his two hounds prevented her. There was nothing we could do!"

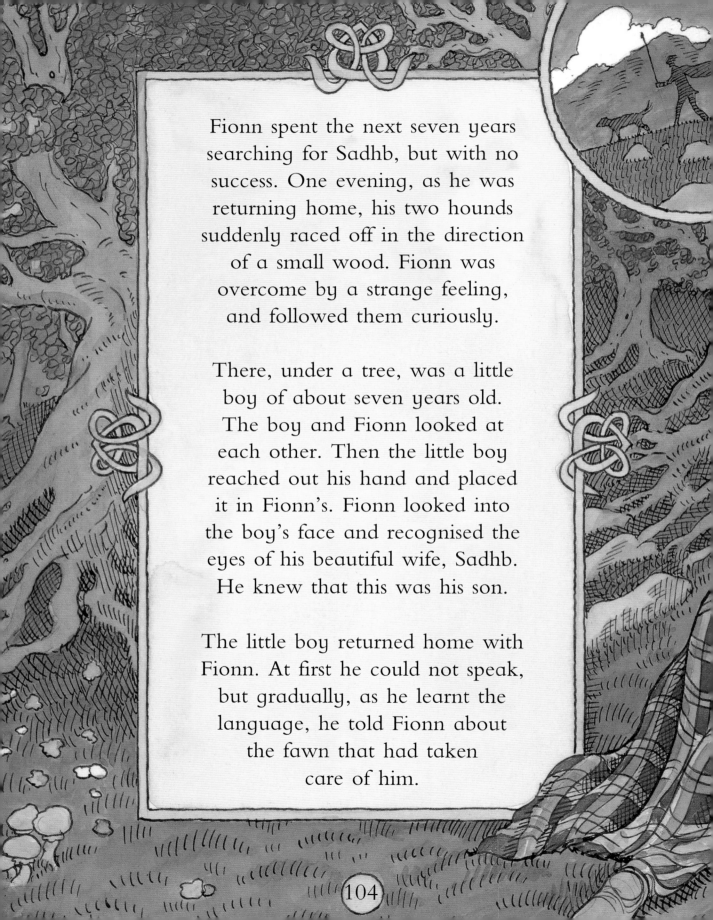

Fionn spent the next seven years searching for Sadhb, but with no success. One evening, as he was returning home, his two hounds suddenly raced off in the direction of a small wood. Fionn was overcome by a strange feeling, and followed them curiously.

There, under a tree, was a little boy of about seven years old. The boy and Fionn looked at each other. Then the little boy reached out his hand and placed it in Fionn's. Fionn looked into the boy's face and recognised the eyes of his beautiful wife, Sadhb. He knew that this was his son.

The little boy returned home with Fionn. At first he could not speak, but gradually, as he learnt the language, he told Fionn about the fawn that had taken care of him.

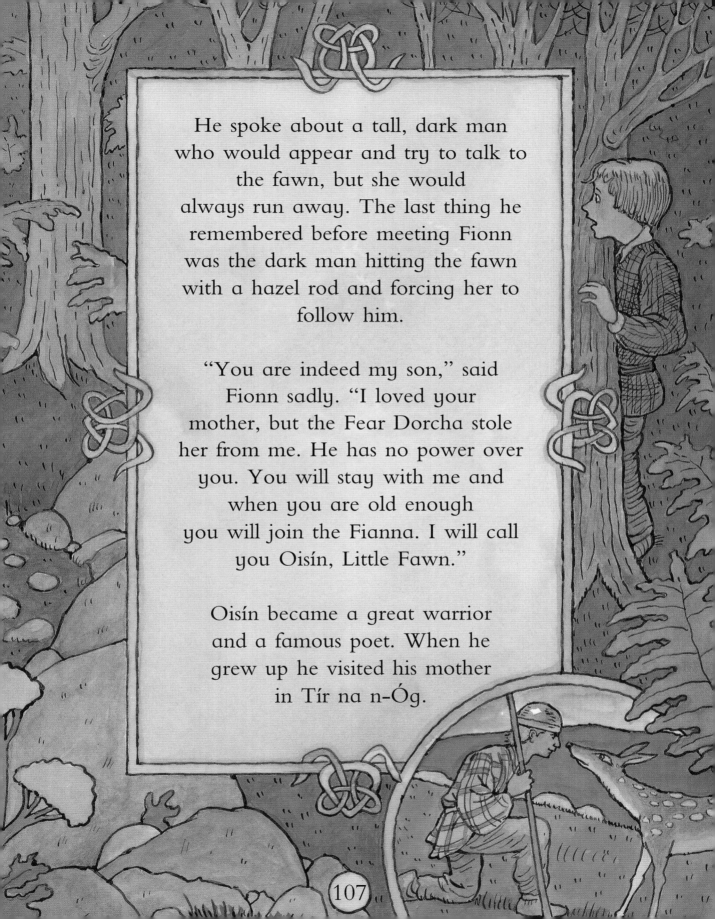

He spoke about a tall, dark man who would appear and try to talk to the fawn, but she would always run away. The last thing he remembered before meeting Fionn was the dark man hitting the fawn with a hazel rod and forcing her to follow him.

"You are indeed my son," said Fionn sadly. "I loved your mother, but the Fear Dorcha stole her from me. He has no power over you. You will stay with me and when you are old enough you will join the Fianna. I will call you Oisín, Little Fawn."

Oisín became a great warrior and a famous poet. When he grew up he visited his mother in Tír na n-Óg.

Children of Lir

Once upon a time there lived a king called Lir who had four children: a daughter named Fionnuala and three sons called Aodh, Fiachra and Con.

Their mother the queen was dead, and the children were sad because they missed her terribly. They missed the stories she used to tell them, the games she used to play, and the songs she sang at bedtime as she hugged them to sleep.

The king saw that his children
were sad and needed a mother,
so he decided to marry again.
His new bride was called
Aoife. She was beautiful, but
she was not the kind-hearted
person the king thought
she was.

Aoife grew jealous of the four
children because their father
loved them very much. She
wanted the king all to herself,
so she planned to get rid of
the children. She asked a
druid to help her,
and together they
thought up a
terrible spell.

In the castle grounds there was a lovely lake which the children spent most of their time playing beside. One day Aoife went with the children to the lakeside. As they played in the water, she suddenly pulled out a magic wand and waved it over them. There was a flash of light, and the children vanished. In their place were four beautiful white swans.

One of the swans opened its beak and spoke with Fionnuala's voice. "Oh, what have you done to us?" she asked, in a frightened voice.

"I have put a spell on you," replied Aoife. "Now everything you have will be mine. You will be swans for nine hundred years. You will spend three hundred years on this lake, three hundred years on the Sea of Moyle and three hundred years on the Isle of Glora. Only the sound of a church bell can break the spell."

When the children did not
come home that evening, the
king went to look for them by
the lake. As he came near,
four swans swam up to him.
He was amazed when they
began to call out.
"Father, father," they cried,
"we are your children. Aoife
has placed a terrible magic
spell on us."

The king ran back to the castle and pleaded with Aoife to change the swans back into children, but she refused. Now he saw how selfish she was and banished her from the kingdom. Lir promised a reward to anyone who could break the spell, but nobody knew how.

Lir spent the rest of his life beside the lake, talking to his children, until he grew old and died. The swans were heartbroken. They no longer talked or sang, and nobody came to see them.

Three hundred years passed
and it was time for the swans
to move to the cold and stormy
Sea of Moyle between Ireland
and Scotland.

The poor swans
were tossed
about by the
wild waves

and dashed against sharp
rocks. It was a harsh life
with little food and the
years passed slowly.

When the time came for them
to fly to the Isle of Glora, the
swans were old and tired.
Although it was warmer on
the island and there was
lots of food, they were still
very lonely.

Then one day they
heard the sound
for which they had waited
nine hundred years.
It was the sound
of a church bell.

The bell was ringing in the tower of a little church. An old man, called Caomhóg, stood outside. He was amazed to hear swans talking and listened to their sad story in astonishment. Then he went inside his church and brought out some holy water which he sprinkled on the swans while he prayed. As soon as the water touched them, the swans miraculously began to change into an old, old woman and three old, old men.

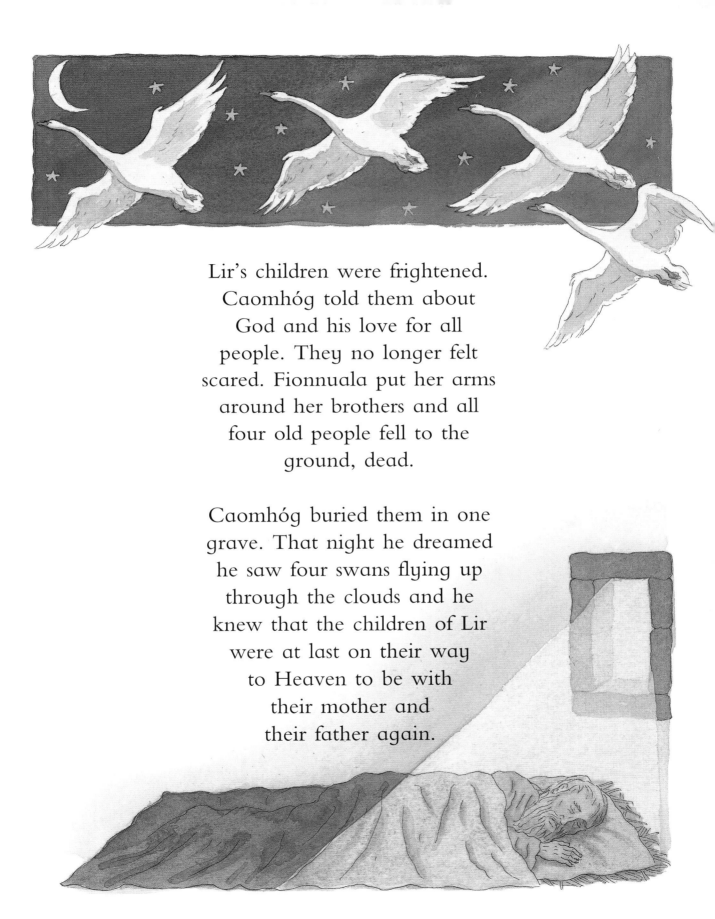

Lir's children were frightened.
Caomhóg told them about
God and his love for all
people. They no longer felt
scared. Fionnuala put her arms
around her brothers and all
four old people fell to the
ground, dead.

Caomhóg buried them in one
grave. That night he dreamed
he saw four swans flying up
through the clouds and he
knew that the children of Lir
were at last on their way
to Heaven to be with
their mother and
their father again.

Brian O'Linn

Brian O'Linn was a gentleman born,
His hair it was long and his beard unshorn,
His teeth were out and his eyes far in –
 "I'm a wonderful beauty," says Brian O'Linn!

Brian O'Linn was hard up for a coat,
He borrowed the skin of a neighbouring goat,
He buckled the horns right under his chin –
"They'll answer for pistols," says Brian O'Linn!

Brian O'Linn had no breeches to wear,
He got him a sheepskin to make him a pair,
With the fleshy side out and the woolly side in –
"They are pleasant and cool," says Brian O'Linn!

Brian O'Linn had no hat to his head,
He stuck on a pot that was under the shed,
He murdered a cod for the sake of his fin –
" 'Twill pass for a feather," says Brian O'Linn!

Brian O'Linn had no shirt to his back,
He went to a neighbour and borrowed a sack,
He puckered a meal-bag under his chin –
"They'll take it for ruffles," says Brian O'Linn!

Brian O'Linn had no shoes at all,
He bought an old pair at a cobbler's stall,
The uppers were broke and the soles were thin –
"They'll do me for dancing," says Brian O'Linn!

Brian O'Linn had no watch to wear,
He bought a fine turnip and scooped it out fair,
He slipped a live cricket right under the skin –
"They'll think it is ticking," says Brian O'Linn!

Brian O'Linn was in want of a brooch,
He stuck a brass pin in a big cockroach,
The breast of his shirt he fixed it straight in –
"They'll think it's a diamond," says Brian O'Linn!

Brian O'Linn went a-courting one night,
He set both the mother and daughter to fight –
"Stop, stop," he exclaimed, "if you have but the tin,
I'll marry you both," says Brian O'Linn!

Brian O'Linn went to bring his wife home,
He had but one horse, that was all skin and bone –
"I'll put her behind me, as nate as a pin,
And her mother before me," says Brian O'Linn!

Brian O'Linn and his wife and wife's mother,
They all crossed over the bridge together,
The bridge broke down, and they all tumbled in –
"We'll go home by water," says Brian O'Linn!

Anonymous

Niamh

Niamh sat up in bed and listened carefully. There it was again! She had heard the sounds before, but this time she decided to investigate. She slipped on her dressing gown and made her way to the bedroom door. Down the stairs she crept. It was difficult to see because the only light to guide her was the light of the full moon that shone through the window. Just as she reached the kitchen door she knew that she was not alone.

It was her brother Liam. "Where are you going?" he whispered. "I heard the music again. This time I'm going to find out who is playing it. You can come with me," she replied. "But only if you do what I tell you." Liam didn't like to be told what to do, but he was a curious little boy and the chance of an adventure was too tempting to miss.

The children stood outside in the silver moonlight and listened. The music seemed no more than a whisper or a rustling of leaves. Was it the fairy people their grandmother had told them about? "Let's follow the path to the clearing in the wood," whispered Niamh. "I think that's where they meet." Liam agreed and they set off into the chilly night, full of excitement — and a little frightened as well.

A faint light flickered in the bushes as they approached the clearing. They could hear music — sweet, light music. Niamh couldn't decide what instruments were playing. She thought she could hear harps and flutes. It seemed as if the music was calling her. "Don't go too close," her brother warned. "Gran said that if the fairy people catch you, they'll keep you. Quick, let's go home."

Niamh crept closer and closer to the light. "Look!" she whispered excitedly. "Look! I was right all along!" Liam peeped through the branches. What a sight it was! Lights twinkled from the trees in the clearing. The children could see little people dancing in the centre. Gran's description of the leprechauns was perfect, right down to the silver buckles on their tiny shoes.

A new dance began with a faster rhythm. The music seemed to call them to join the dance. Liam remembered his Gran's warning to cover his ears. Niamh was spellbound. She began to move in time with the music. Suddenly there was a flash of light and Liam was blinded for a moment. When he opened his eyes again he was alone and his sister had vanished.

The search for Niamh went on for
a long time but there was not a
trace of her to be found.

Early one morning, many years later, Liam returned to the clearing in the wood. Although he now lived far away, he visited the spot where his sister had disappeared whenever he could.

As he approached he heard a child calling, "Liam! Liam! Where are you? We must go home." The voice was familiar. A little girl ran up to him and asked "Have you seen my brother? We were dancing with the fairies and the leprechauns for twenty minutes and he's wandered off! It's time we went home."

Liam stared at her in amazement. "Niamh," he said, "Is it really you? You haven't spent twenty minutes dancing, you've been away for twenty years!"

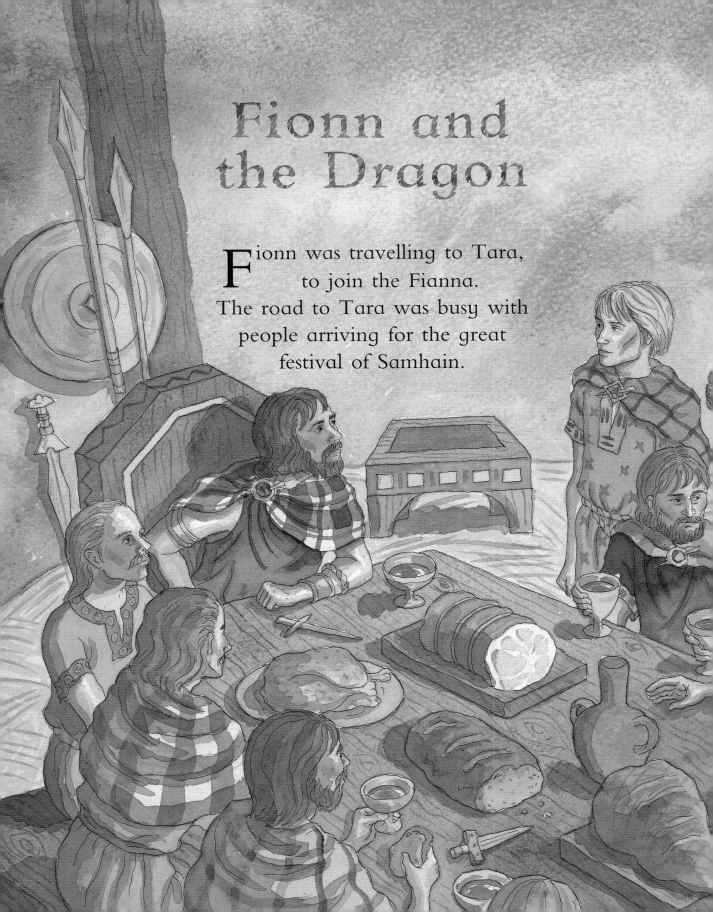

Fionn and the Dragon

Fionn was travelling to Tara, to join the Fianna. The road to Tara was busy with people arriving for the great festival of Samhain.

Fionn arrived in time for the feast
but there was no seat for him in
the banqueting hall.
"Who are you?" the High King
asked. "I don't recognise you.
Tell me your name."
"I am Fionn, the son of
Cumhall," said the young man.
There was silence in the great
hall. All eyes were on Goll Mac
Morna, the man who had killed
Fionn's father, Cumhall.
The king spoke.
"You are the son of a friend and
you are welcome to my feast."
He put Fionn next to his own sons
and the feast began.

During the feast the High
King spoke.
"For the past nine years Tara has
been visited on the festival of
Samhain by an evil spirit. This
spirit appears in the form of a
fire-breathing dragon which
causes great damage.

My magicians are powerless.
Many warriors have tried to kill
it but all have failed. Is there
anyone among you who will save
Tara?" the High King asked.
No one spoke. Fionn stood up.
"What reward will be given
to the person who is
successful?" he asked.
"I will grant you whatever you
want," replied the king.
"In that case I will defend Tara
from the evil spirit," said Fionn.

135

Fionn walked to the outer walls
of the city. The sky was dark
and there was no sound to be
heard. The people were
gathered safely inside the walls.
Fionn heard footsteps.

"Who goes there?" he called.
"I am a friend," came the reply.
"I was a friend of your father's
and I have come to repay a
favour your father did for me.
As you know, when the dragon
approaches, he plays sweet music.
Anyone who hears this music
falls asleep at once. Take this
magic spear and, as soon as the
music begins, press it against
your forehead and the music
will have no power over you.
I must hurry away now."
Fionn was left alone.

From the darkness came a low, sweet sound. It was the magic music of the Fairyworld. Immediately Fionn put the spear to his forehead and although the people of Tara fell into a deep sleep, Fionn remained awake. The dragon breathed a long blue flame. Fionn aimed and fired the spear. The dragon fell dead on the spot. Fionn cut off its head.

"What is your wish?" the High
King asked.
"I ask to be the leader of the Fianna
as my father was," replied the
proud hero.
The High King agreed.

"You have a choice to make,"
the High King said to Goll Mac
Morna. "You can accept Fionn
as your leader or you must
leave Ireland."

Goll thought for a while and then
spoke to Fionn.
"Here is my hand. I will gladly
serve you."
Once Goll Mac Morna had
submitted, the other warriors of
the Fianna followed. So Fionn
became their leader, as his father
before him had been.

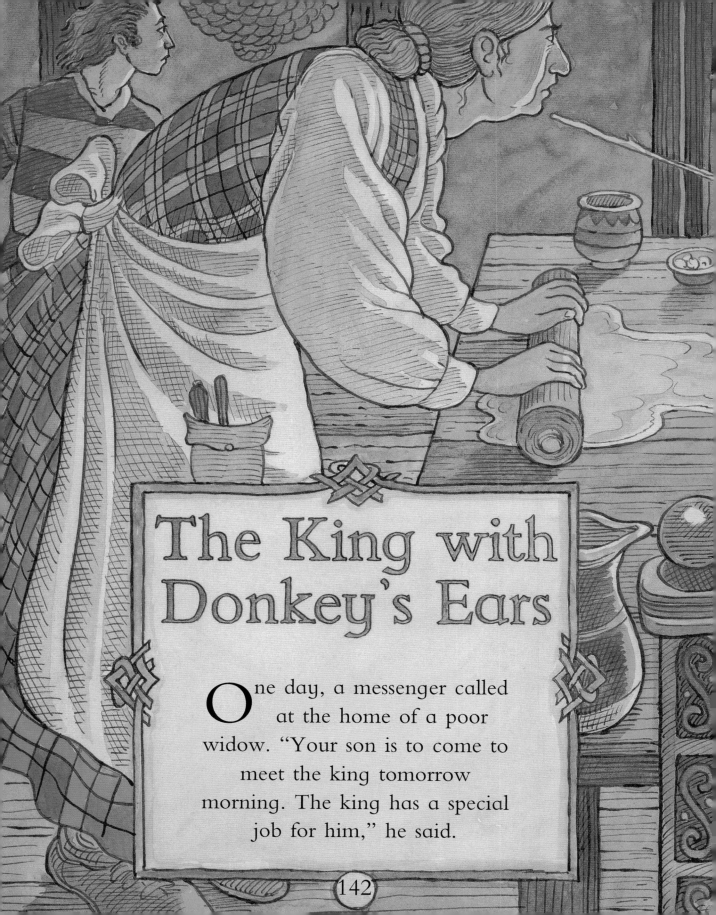

The King with Donkey's Ears

One day, a messenger called at the home of a poor widow. "Your son is to come to meet the king tomorrow morning. The king has a special job for him," he said.

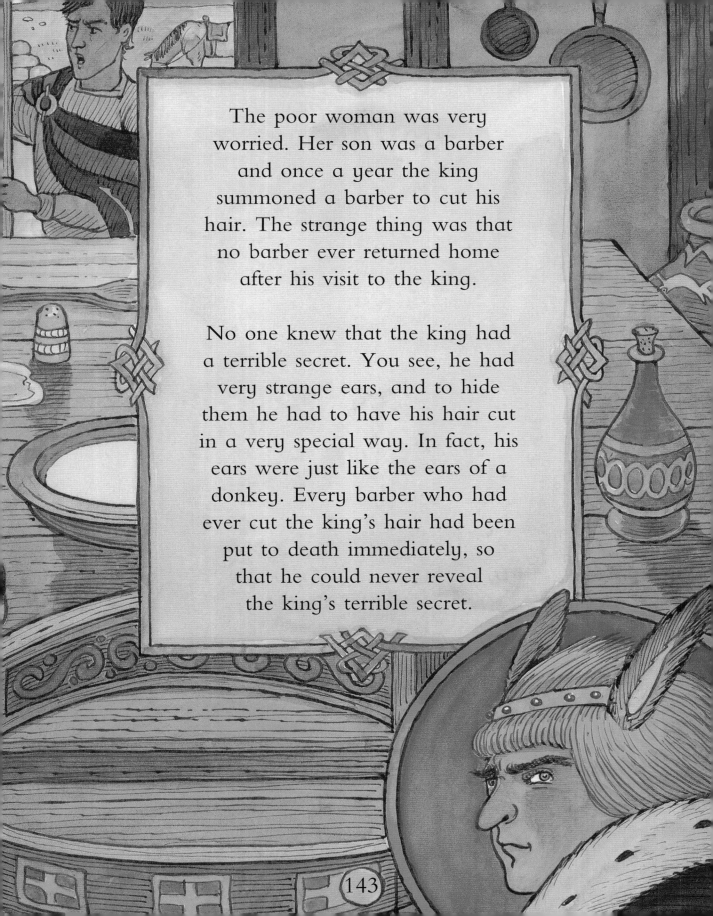

The poor woman was very worried. Her son was a barber and once a year the king summoned a barber to cut his hair. The strange thing was that no barber ever returned home after his visit to the king.

No one knew that the king had a terrible secret. You see, he had very strange ears, and to hide them he had to have his hair cut in a very special way. In fact, his ears were just like the ears of a donkey. Every barber who had ever cut the king's hair had been put to death immediately, so that he could never reveal the king's terrible secret.

The woman made her way to see the king. "My son is all that I have in the world," she cried. "Please do not kill my son. If he dies I will have no one to care for me."

The king was sorry for the old woman and he thought for a while. "I will agree to spare his life on one condition," he replied. "Your son must promise never to tell any living person about anything he sees while he is in my castle." Next day the son arrived to cut the king's hair. Imagine his surprise when he saw the king's ears! However, he was a clever boy and he knew that his life depended on his keeping the secret, so he said nothing.

As time passed his mother noticed that her son was unwell. He could not sleep nor eat. There seemed to be something troubling him, but when she questioned him he would not answer.

She decided to send for a druid. "I cannot help him," the druid said. "He knows a terrible secret. He has promised not to tell any living person his secret, but unless he tells it he will not get better."

The wise druid thought for a while. "I have a solution to the problem. He must go into the forest and find the tall willow tree that grows beside the stream. If he whispers the secret to the leaves, the promise will not be broken because he will not have told any living person."

The boy did as he was told and immediately he felt as if a heavy weight was lifted from his shoulders.

That was not the end of the story. Some days later the king's harper went to cut some wood for a new harp.

That night, when he began to play for the king and the other chieftains, a strange music came from the harp.

"The king, the king, has donkey's ears, has donkey's ears," it sang.

The secret was revealed. At first
the king was terrified, but when
he saw that no one was afraid of
him, or laughed at him, he knew
that he would never have to hide
his donkey's ears again.

149

Herrings

Be not sparing,
Leave off swearing.
Buy my herring
Fresh from Malahide,
Better never was tried.
Come, eat them with pure fresh butter and mustard,
Their bellies are soft, and as white as a custard.
Come, sixpence a dozen, to get me some bread,
Or, like my own herrings, I soon shall be dead.

Jonathan Swift

A Riddle

We are little airy creatures,
All of different voice and features,
One of us in glass is set,
One of us you'll find in jet,
T'other you may see in tin,
And the fourth a box within,
If the fifth you should pursue
It can never fly from you.

Jonathan Swift

Hold this up to a mirror to find the answer:

the vowels

Setanta

Seven year old Setanta was determined to become a member of the famous Red Branch Knights of Ulster. His father, the King of Dundalk, had told him about the special school in Armagh, called the Macra, for the young boys who would one day join the brave warriors.

Setanta pleaded with his parents to let him go there but they refused.

"You are much too young,
Setanta. Wait a little longer
and then we will allow you to
go," they said.

Setanta decided he could not
wait any longer and so one
day he set off for Armagh.
It was a long journey but
Setanta had his hurley and
sliotar to play with. He hit
the sliotar far ahead and ran
forward to catch it on his
hurley stick before it hit
the ground.

When Setanta reached the
castle of King Connor at
Armagh he found the hundred
and fifty boys of the Macra
gathered on the great plain in
front of the castle. Some of
them were playing hurling and
as this was his favourite game
he hurried over to join in.
Almost immediately he scored
a brilliant goal.

The other boys were furious
that this young boy had joined
their game uninvited and they
attacked him.

Setanta fought bravely. The noise disturbed the king who was playing chess. He sent a servant outside to see what was happening. Setanta was brought before the king.

"I am Setanta, son of the King of Dundalk, your brother. I have come all this way to join the Macra because I want to become one of the Red Branch Knights as soon as I am old enough." The king liked Setanta's brave words and welcomed him to the Macra.

Time passed quickly for Setanta. He loved his new life at the Macra.

One day, Culann, the blacksmith who made spears and swords for Connor, invited the king, his knights and Setanta to a feast.

When it was time to set off
for the feast, Setanta was
playing a game of hurling. He
told the king that he would
follow as soon as the game
was finished. The feast began
and Connor forgot to mention
that Setanta would be joining
the party later. Thinking all
his guests had arrived, the
blacksmith unchained his
wolfhound which guarded his
house each night.

As soon as the game was over
Setanta set out. When he
arrived at Culann's house he
heard the deep growls of the
wolfhound. Suddenly the
hound leapt forward out of
the dark to attack. Setanta
saw the sharp teeth bared.
With all his strength Setanta
hurled a sliotar down the
hound's throat. Then he
caught the animal by its hind
legs and dashed it against a
rock. With a loud groan
the wolfhound fell
down, dead.

Inside, the feast party had
heard the dog growling.
"My nephew, Setanta," Connor
cried. "I forgot about him!"
He and the Red Branch
Knights rushed out, expecting
to find the young boy torn
to pieces.

Connor was amazed and
delighted to find his nephew
alive and he was proud of his
great strength.

Culann was relieved that the
boy was safe but he was sad
that he had lost the wolfhound
he loved which had faithfully
guarded his house every night.

"Let me take the place of your
hound until I have trained one
of its puppies," said Setanta.
Culann agreed. From that day
on, Setanta was called Cú
Chulainn which means the
Hound of Culann.

The Fairy Lios

One afternoon in early summer, Eithne and her brother Connor were playing in the field behind their house. Eithne was busy making daisy chains and then she decided to pick some of the wild flowers that were growing in the field. Her favourites were the bluebells. "Don't pick the flowers from the fairy lios, Eithne, or you will be sorry," her brother warned.

Eithne ignored his warning and
continued to pick bluebells from
the centre of the lios. "There are
so many growing here that the
fairies couldn't possibly notice if a
few were picked," she answered.

The children returned home and
Eithne put the bluebells in a vase
on the kitchen table. As soon as
their mother heard that she had
picked them from the lios, she
rushed outside and put them on
the window ledge. She knew that
if the fairy people were angry
Eithne might be punished for
interfering with the lios. And so
she was!

After Eithne lay down in bed
that night she jumped up
screaming. Her bed was full of
nettles! She tried to sleep in her
parents' bed, but as soon as she
lay down it too was full of
stinging nettles. She tried
Connor's bed but the same thing
happened. "I'm sorry I ever went
near the lios," she cried.

Her parents went to visit a wise old woman who lived nearby, to ask what they should do. "The fairies will not be easy to please," she said. "But if someone in your family could do a good deed for them, perhaps they might remove the nettles."

The family thought and thought but what could they possibly do for the fairy people? At last, Connor had an idea. That night, he crept out of the house and went to the lios.

At midnight the lights twinkled in
the lios and he could hear soft,
light music. Connor loved music
and he could play all sorts of tunes
on his feadóg (tin whistle). He
recognised some of these tunes and
thought to himself that it was
strange that the little people should
have the same music as mortals.

Cautiously, he pulled back the
bushes and there in front of him
were fairies and leprechauns
dancing merrily! "The leprechaun
has a whistle just like mine,"
he thought.

When the music stopped Connor moved forward. There was silence, then one of the leprechauns spoke angrily. "Your sister disturbed our lios and now you have come to disturb our dance." "No, no," said Connor. "I have come to tell you how sorry she is. I promise that she will never do such a thing again. Please take the nettles from her bed and let her sleep."

"Impossible!" said the leprechaun. "Go away before we punish you too." He turned to the musician. "Let the music start again!"

Connor stood outside the lios feeling very sad. It seemed that there was nothing to be done. His sister would never be able to sleep in a bed again. Then he had another idea.

Connor listened to the music once more. When the next dance was over and he thought that the piper was resting, he began to play a soft, sad tune. Playing his tune all the while, he parted the bushes and stepped into the lios. This time the fairy people listened.

He played for what seemed to be forever and when he finished, not a sound was to be heard. Then the applause began and the leprechaun who had spoken earlier spoke again. "Well played, Connor. You are a brave young man. We must reward you."
"Oh no, I don't want anything for myself. I just want help for my sister Eithne."

The leprechaun turned to the others. They nodded. "Return home," he said. "We will grant your wish." Dawn broke and in an instant the lios was emptied as the Sidhe vanished.

When Connor returned home, he found Eithne fast asleep in bed. His family knew that Connor had somehow broken the spell but they also knew that they could never ask how.

173

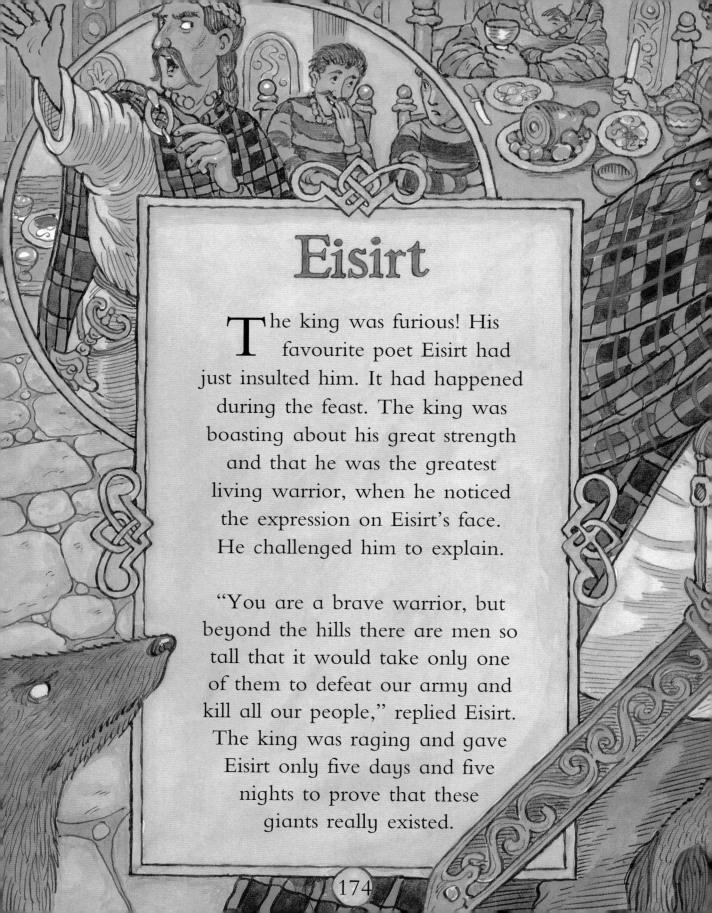

Eisirt

The king was furious! His favourite poet Eisirt had just insulted him. It had happened during the feast. The king was boasting about his great strength and that he was the greatest living warrior, when he noticed the expression on Eisirt's face. He challenged him to explain.

"You are a brave warrior, but beyond the hills there are men so tall that it would take only one of them to defeat our army and kill all our people," replied Eisirt. The king was raging and gave Eisirt only five days and five nights to prove that these giants really existed.

174

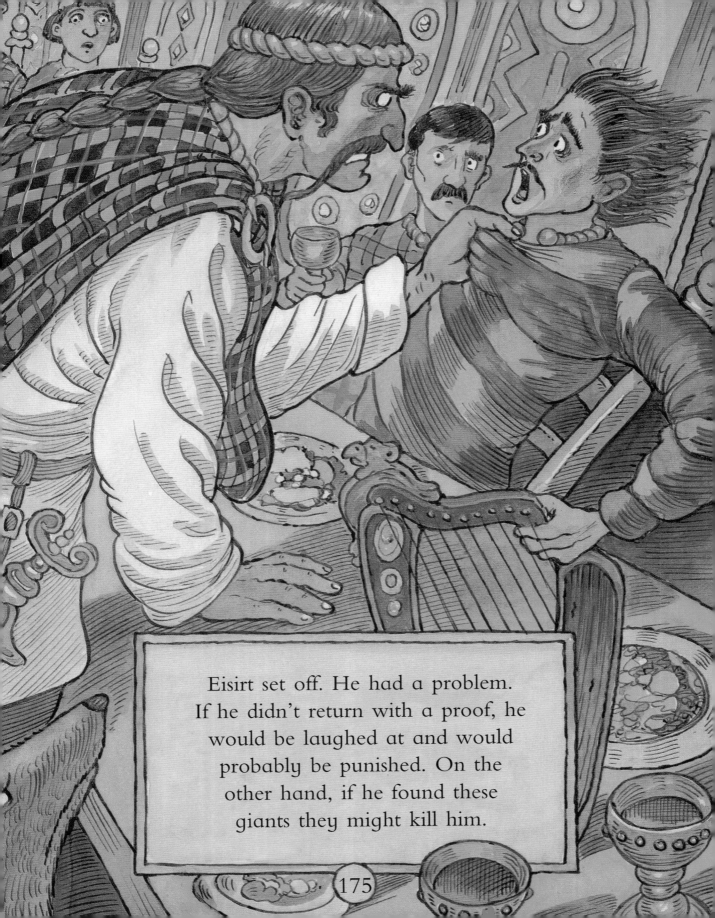

Eisirt set off. He had a problem. If he didn't return with a proof, he would be laughed at and would probably be punished. On the other hand, if he found these giants they might kill him.

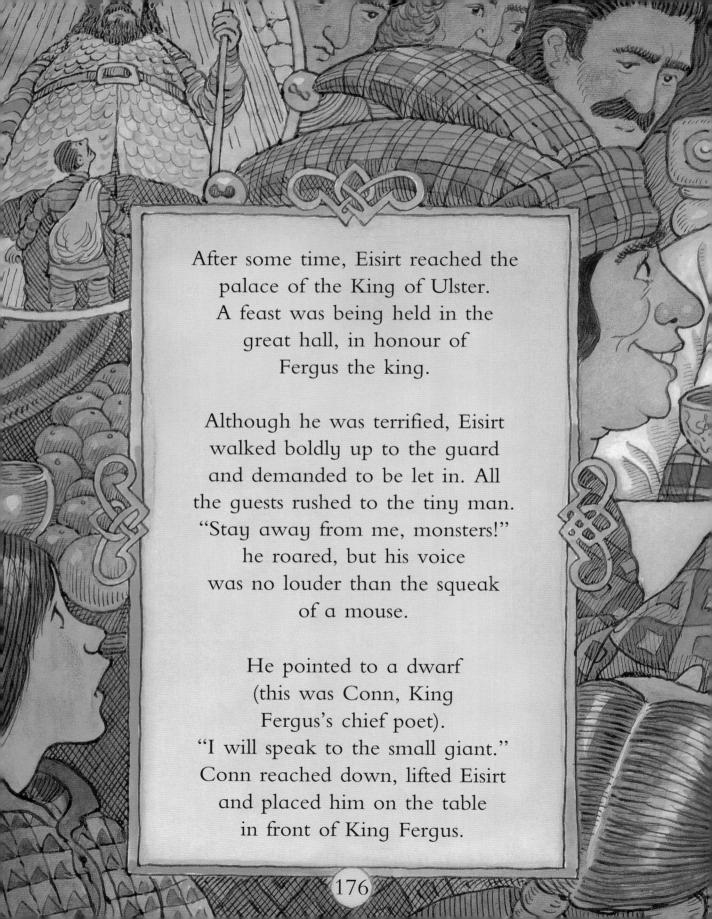

After some time, Eisirt reached the
palace of the King of Ulster.
A feast was being held in the
great hall, in honour of
Fergus the king.

Although he was terrified, Eisirt
walked boldly up to the guard
and demanded to be let in. All
the guests rushed to the tiny man.
"Stay away from me, monsters!"
he roared, but his voice
was no louder than the squeak
of a mouse.

He pointed to a dwarf
(this was Conn, King
Fergus's chief poet).
"I will speak to the small giant."
Conn reached down, lifted Eisirt
and placed him on the table
in front of King Fergus.

"Who are you, little man, and
where do you come from?"
asked the king.
"I am Eisirt, chief poet and wise
man of my people."
"You are very welcome here,"
said Fergus. "You must join us,
and after you have eaten,
you must sing for us and tell us
about your home."

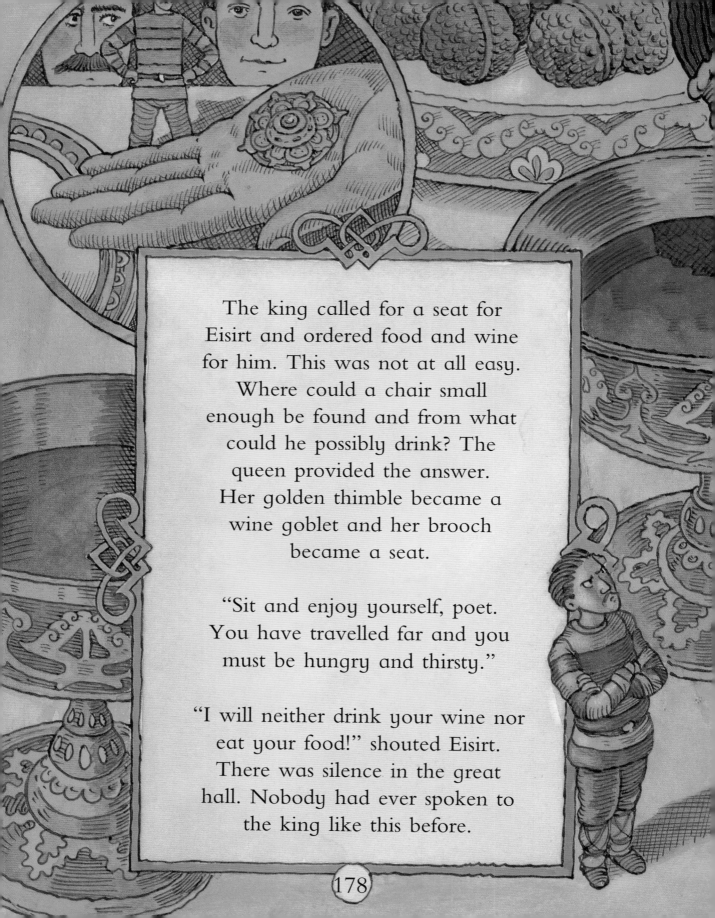

The king called for a seat for
Eisirt and ordered food and wine
for him. This was not at all easy.
Where could a chair small
enough be found and from what
could he possibly drink? The
queen provided the answer.
Her golden thimble became a
wine goblet and her brooch
became a seat.

"Sit and enjoy yourself, poet.
You have travelled far and you
must be hungry and thirsty."

"I will neither drink your wine nor
eat your food!" shouted Eisirt.
There was silence in the great
hall. Nobody had ever spoken to
the king like this before.

Suddenly the king laughed.
"Oh dear, why are you so angry
with me? If I am not careful you
might challenge me to a duel,
and what chance would I have
against such bravery as yours?"

"I will put you in my goblet,
then you will have to drink!"
With that, he lifted Eisirt
and dropped him into
a goblet of wine.

The little man tried to swim. "King Fergus of Ulster, you are doing a foolish thing. If I drown, you will never hear about my wonderful home or where it is." "Save him! Save him!" the guests cried out. Fergus took him out.

"Why did you insult us by refusing our hospitality?"

"If I told you," answered Eisirt, "you would be very angry with me. I don't think that people who make you angry live very long."

"I give you my word that I will listen to what you have to say and that you will not be harmed," answered the king.

"Well," said Eisirt, "I cannot stand injustice, and I know that you are unjust to your chief steward. I also know that he is cheating you! I cannot eat or drink here while this is happening."

There was silence in the great hall. This was treason. No one spoke to the king like this!

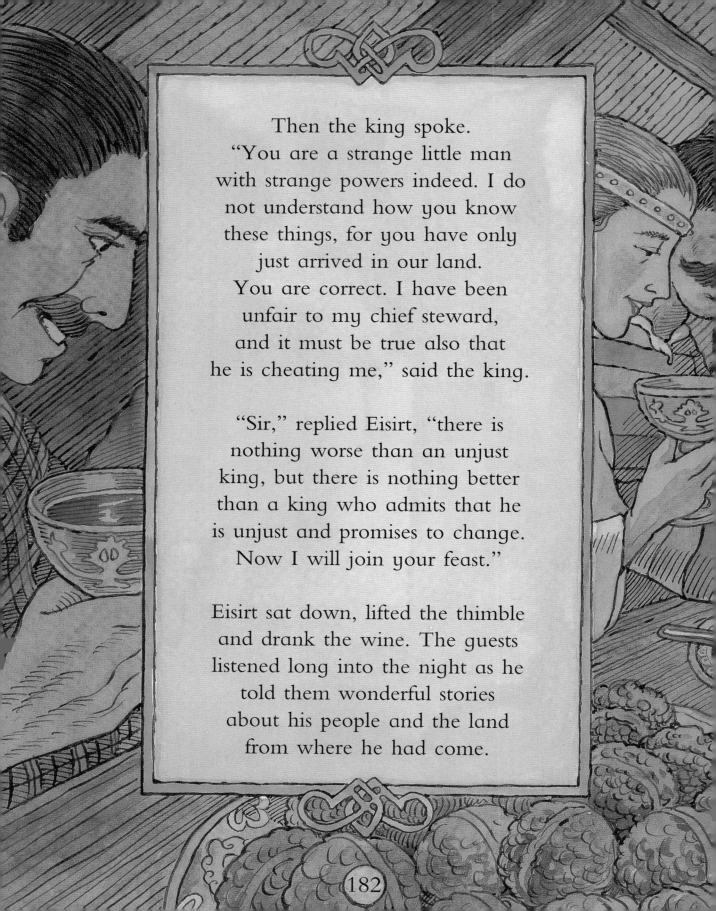

Then the king spoke.
"You are a strange little man
with strange powers indeed. I do
not understand how you know
these things, for you have only
just arrived in our land.
You are correct. I have been
unfair to my chief steward,
and it must be true also that
he is cheating me," said the king.

"Sir," replied Eisirt, "there is
nothing worse than an unjust
king, but there is nothing better
than a king who admits that he
is unjust and promises to change.
Now I will join your feast."

Eisirt sat down, lifted the thimble
and drank the wine. The guests
listened long into the night as he
told them wonderful stories
about his people and the land
from where he had come.

The Fairies

Up the airy mountain,
Down the rushy glen,
We daren't go a-hunting
For fear of little men;
Wee folk, good folk,
Trooping all together;
Green jacket, red cap,
And white owl's feather!

Down along the rocky shore
Some make their home –
They live on crispy pancakes
Of yellow tide-foam;
Some in the reeds
Of the black mountain lake,
With frogs for their watch-dogs,
All night awake.

High on the hilltop
The old king sits;
He is now so old and grey,
He's nigh lost his wits.

With a bridge of white mist
Columbkill he crosses
On his stately journeys
From Slieveleague to Rosses;
Or going up with music
On cold, starry
nights,

To sup with the Queen
Of the gay Northern Lights.

They stole little Bridget
For seven years long;
When she came down again
Her friends were all gone.
They took her lightly back,
Between the night and morrow,
They thought that she
was fast asleep,
But she was dead with sorrow.
They have kept her ever since
Deep within the lake,
On a bed of flag-leaves,
Watching till she wake.

By the craggy hillside,
Through the mosses bare,
They have planted thorn-trees
For pleasure here and there.
If any man so daring
As dig one up in spite,
He shall find their sharpest thorns
In his bed at night.

Up the airy mountain,
Down the rushy glen,
We daren't go a-hunting
For fear of little men;
Wee folk, good folk,
Trooping all together;
Green jacket,
red cap,
And white
owl's feather!

William Allingham

Pronunciation guide

Áinle	awn-le
Aodh	ay
Aoife	ee-fa
Avourneen	a-vore-neen
Binn Éadair	bin ay-dir
Caoilte Mac Rónáin	kweel-cha mac row-nawn
Caomhóg	kay-vogue
Conán Maol	con-awn mw-ayl
Cú Chulainn	coo kullen
Eithne	eth-ne
Eoin	owe-in
Feidhlim	fay-lim
Fiachra	fee-a-cra
Fianna	fee-a-na
Finnéigeas	fin-ay-gas
Fionnuala	fin-oo-la
Gleann na Smól	glen-ass-mole
Hill of Howth	hill of hoe-th
Leabharcham	lee-ow-er-come
Lios	lis

Lir	leer
Maeve	mayve
Naoise	nee-sha
Niamh	nee–uv
Oisín	ush-een
Sadhb	sigh-v
Samhain	sow-in (rhyme sow with cow)
Sceolán	skull-awn
Sidhe	she
Sliabh Bloom	sleeve bloom
Slieveleague	sleeve league
Tír na n-Óg	tier ne nogue
Uisneach	ish-knock

Biographies

Fiona Waters has published a number of very successful anthologies and is well known in the book world for her unparalleled understanding of children's books. She has compiled many poetry collections which introduce children to the magical world of imagery, make-believe and contemporary life.

Yvonne Carroll is a children's writer with considerable knowledge of Irish legends and folklore. She retells traditional stories with clarity and verve, and brings to life the beauty, mystery and fun of much-loved and familiar characters and their exploits.

Cecil Frances Alexander (1818-95) was born in County Wicklow but lived in the North of Ireland for most of her life. As a Sunday School teacher in Strabane, she wrote several now-famous hymns.

Robert Dwyer Joyce (1830-83) was born in Glenosheen, County Limerick. He trained first as a teacher, then qualified as a doctor, and in 1866 he emigrated to Boston. He continued to write in the United States and returned to Ireland shortly before his death.

Jonathan Swift (1667-1745) was born in Dublin. He is acknowledged as the greatest satirist in the English language, and is best remembered as the author of *Gulliver's Travels*. In 1713, he became the Dean of St Patrick's Cathedral in Dublin.

William Allingham (1824-89) was born in Ballyshannon, County Donegal. He worked as a customs officer, while writing his poems at night. In 1870, he moved to London and forged friendships with Thomas Carlyle and Alfred, Lord Tennyson.

Book information

A Child's Treasury of Irish Stories & Poems

These stories and poems are taken from the following books published by Gill & Macmillan

Irish Legends for Children retold by Yvonne Carroll
Illustrated by Lucy Su
Copyright © 1994 Zigzag Publishing Ltd
Deirdre of the Sorrows
The Salmon of Knowledge
Children of Lir
Fionn and the Dragon
Setanta

Great Irish Legends for Children retold by Yvonne Carroll
Illustrated by Robin Lawrie
Copyright © 1994 Zigzag Publishing Ltd
The Beggarman
The Giant from Scotland
Oisín
The King with Donkey's Ears
Eisirt

Leprechaun Tales retold by Yvonne Carroll
Illustrated by Jacqueline East
Copyright © 1999 Tony Potter Publishing Ltd
The Crock of Gold
The Sidhe
The Magic Cloak
Niamh
The Fairy Lios

Irish Poems — A Collection for Children
Selected by Fiona Waters
Illustrated by Peter Rutherford
Copyright © 2001 Tony Potter Publishing Ltd
A Ballad of Master McGrath
All Things Bright and Beautiful
Cockles and Mussels
The Leprahaun
Brian O'Linn
Herrings
A Riddle
The Fairies